The Eagle's Song

A Tale from the Pacific Northwest

Adapted and Illustrated by

Kristina Rodanas

Little, Brown and Company
Boston   New York   Toronto   London

For Greg, who met me on the river and sang the first song
Special thanks to my editor, Stephanie True, the other half of the team

First Edition

Library of Congress Cataloging-in-Publication Data
Rodanas, Kristina.
    The eagle's song : a tale from the Pacific Northwest / adapted and illustrated by Kristina Rodanas.
    — 1st ed.
        p.   cm.
    Summary: While trying to find his brothers, Ermine encounters an Eagle-man and
his ancient mother, who help him teach the people living on the coast of the Pacific
Northwest how to overcome their isolation and experience the joy of life.
    ISBN 0-316-75375-0
    1. Indians of North America — Northwest Coast of North America — Folklore.
2. Tales — Northwest Coast of North America.
[1. Indians of North America — Northwest, Pacific — Folklore. 2. Folklore — North America.]
I. Title.
E78.N78R59   1995
398.2′09795′04528916 — dc20
[E]   94-6596

10 9 8 7 6 5 4 3 2 1 SC

Published simultaneously in Canada by Little, Brown & Company (Canada) Limited
and in Great Britain by Little, Brown and Company (UK) Limited

Paintings done in colored pencil over watercolor wash. Text set in Adobe Garamond by Typographic House
and display lines set in Tiepolo by Typographic House.

Printed in Hong Kong

Author's Note

The Eagle's Song was inspired by a Native American tale from the Pacific Northwest recorded in Knud Rasmussen's *The Eagle's Gift* (1932, Doubleday, Doran & Company, Inc., Garden City, New York). I hope the story will bring joy to all its readers, and that this joy will be shared by all.

Long, long ago, a group of people lived in a majestic land of light and darkness. Their gray huts all faced the sea, but they were separated by thick forests, so neighbors never gathered together or even spoke to one another. Only the sounds of the waves on the shore broke the stillness. Like a thick fog that dims the sun, loneliness filled their lives, and their hearts turned as cold as the wilderness around them.

In one of the houses, there dwelled three brothers. The two eldest youths were skilled hunters. Their hard work provided plenty of meat and furs, enough to feed and clothe themselves and others many times over. But since all the families kept to themselves, they never thought to share their supplies.

Ermine, the youngest brother, rarely joined the hunt. Instead, he carved bowls and built boxes to hold the food and clothing his brothers supplied. By the dim light of the seal-oil lamp, he decorated his creations with paintings of animals. His brothers shook their heads at the pains he took, but he continued to draw, for it comforted him while they were out hunting.

One day, the older boys left home to stalk mountain goats. Many days passed, but they did not return.

Under shadows of clouds and sun, Ermine set out to search for his brothers. Ice crackled and snapped beneath his feet, and a fierce wind howled through the treetops. Suddenly Ermine heard a low, rhythmic throbbing that filled the air around him. The slow beat grew steadily stronger as Ermine walked deeper into the forest, following the strange sound.

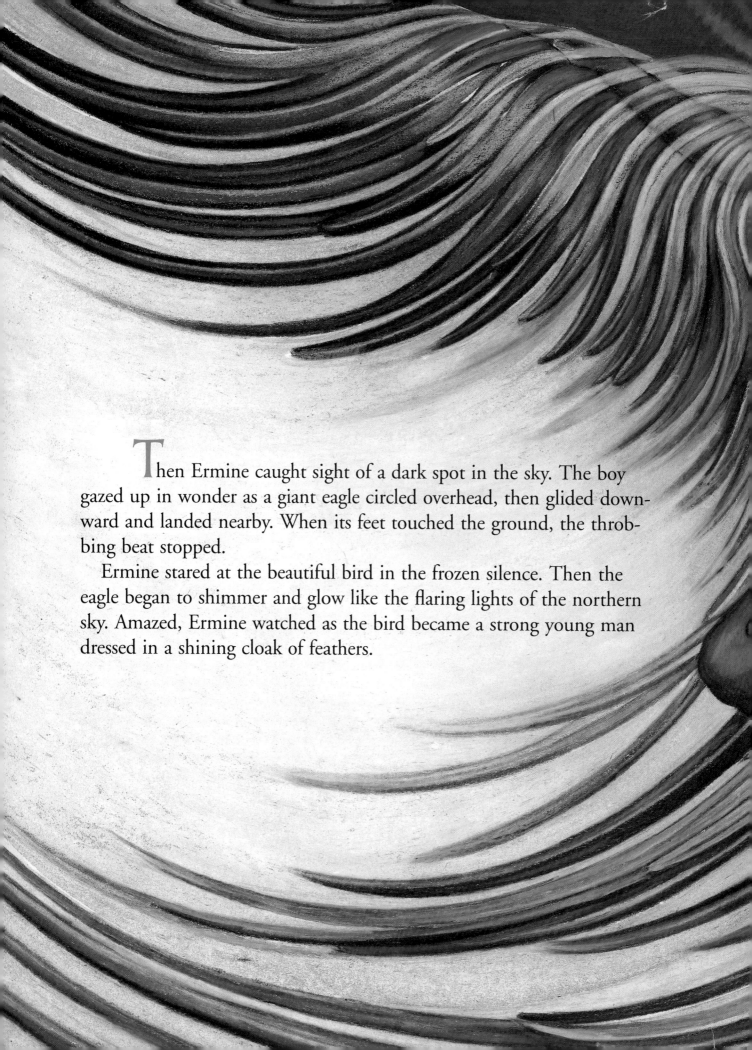

Then Ermine caught sight of a dark spot in the sky. The boy gazed up in wonder as a giant eagle circled overhead, then glided downward and landed nearby. When its feet touched the ground, the throbbing beat stopped.

Ermine stared at the beautiful bird in the frozen silence. Then the eagle began to shimmer and glow like the flaring lights of the northern sky. Amazed, Ermine watched as the bird became a strong young man dressed in a shining cloak of feathers.

The young man approached the boy and said, "My heartbeat led your brothers to this spot. They tried to claim my feathers as a trophy. Do you seek to decorate your weapons with my feathers, too?"

"I am not a hunter," replied Ermine. "I wish only to find my brothers."

"When your brothers tried to harm me, they were changed into rivers as icy as their hearts. I cannot bring them back. But your spirit is different from theirs. If you promise to listen and learn from a heart wiser than mine, you might find the key to releasing them."

Ermine wondered at the eagle-man's words but answered, "I promise."

"Come with me. My mother has much to teach you," said the eagle-man.

In a blaze of light, the man changed back into an eagle. Ermine climbed onto his back, and together they soared over the mountains.

When they landed, the eagle-man guided Ermine into a hall larger than any hut he had ever seen. An ancient woman wrapped in a heavy feathered robe sat in a corner near a roaring fire. As Ermine looked into her tired eyes, he heard the beating of the mother eagle's heart. But the strange throbbing was much fainter than the one he had heard in the forest.

The old woman gave him a bowl heaped high with meat. As he ate, she spoke in a soft voice. "I offer you food, and you accept. Why is this simple gesture unknown to your brothers and all your people? Why do they not rejoice together in all that nature has given them?" She shook her head. "Like a cave of ice that shuts out the light of the sun and the sound of the wind, you and your people isolate yourselves in dark silence."

"But how can we break this silence?" Ermine asked.

From beneath her feathered cloak, the mother eagle pulled a hollow log with caribou skin stretched on either end. "By learning how to celebrate life the way the birds and animals do — with sounds and movements that honor the earth and all that it offers. Listen and learn," she said. She beat on the skin with a short stick, and it made a low, thrumming sound. Then in a tone that matched its rhythm, she murmured, "Why does the sea lion bark at the surf? Why does the otter slide down the waterfall? Why do eagles soar on the wind?"

As the drum's cadence filled his ears, Ermine thought about the birds and animals the old mother spoke of. A strange glow of lightness came over him. He began to move with the music, fluttering his arms like the wings of a raven and stamping his feet like a deer pawing in the snow. Then, following the rhythm of the old mother's drum, Ermine sang his first song:

> *Wind blows outside, fierce and chill,*
> *I hear the wolves howl from the hill,*
> *Raven soars through midnight sky,*
> *But I am warm with friends close by.*

The music faded in the large hall, but Ermine's heart filled with a happiness he longed to share. With a nod of her gray head, the mother eagle motioned to her son that it was time for Ermine to return home. As the young eagle, with Ermine on his back, dove off the mountainside into the icy mist, the old mother called out, "When your people have learned to use the gift of song to break their silence, your brothers will be released. And then I will receive my gift in return."

Their journey came to an end at the place they had met. The eagle-man pressed a fistful of feathers from his shining cloak into Ermine's hand, then flew away. Ermine hurried home and set to work making a drum. He crafted the instrument from wood and caribou hide, and he decorated a cedar branch with the eagle's feathers for a drumstick. When he beat on the drum, it vibrated with a deep throbbing noise that sounded like the beating of the mother eagle's heart.

Pleased with his work, Ermine carried the drum and several boxes and bowls of food outside. Then he sat down to play. Rhythmic tones echoed through the air that separated the people's huts.

The children were the first to hear the drumbeats. Curious, they followed the unfamiliar sounds until they found Ermine and his drum. They crowded silently around him. Faster and faster he struck the drum, until it seemed the children's own hearts beat in harmony with the rhythm.

While Ermine played, he began to sing of the beauty in nature. The cries of animals and birds, the rushing of rivers, and the sighing of winds wove through his melody. Soon the sounds of laughing children intertwined with his song. They chanted and danced with him.

Meanwhile, the hunters returned from the forests and the fishermen came in from the sea. Alarmed by the strange sounds, the men and women followed them to their source. The children welcomed their parents with joyful cries and bowls filled with good things to eat.

The men and women looked at their laughing children in astonishment. But the warm food, the drum's steady beat, and the words of Ermine's songs soon worked their magic. The music loosened their tongues and set their feet stamping rhythmically, until they, too, joined in the merriment and feasting.

As dusk deepened into night, the winds carried the echoing music throughout the land. The animals and birds heard the sounds and felt their magic. In pairs, all kinds of creatures gathered along the shore near Ermine's hut. Wolves, ravens, hawks, and seals sang their own songs while elk and bears danced among them.

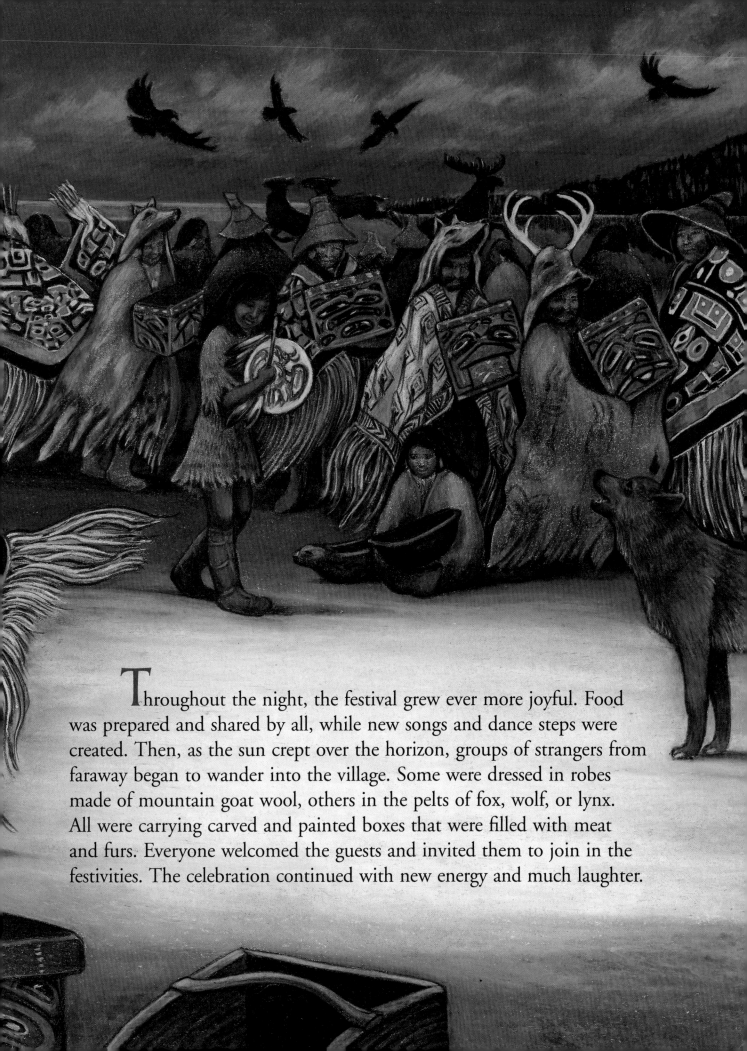

Throughout the night, the festival grew ever more joyful. Food was prepared and shared by all, while new songs and dance steps were created. Then, as the sun crept over the horizon, groups of strangers from faraway began to wander into the village. Some were dressed in robes made of mountain goat wool, others in the pelts of fox, wolf, or lynx. All were carrying carved and painted boxes that were filled with meat and furs. Everyone welcomed the guests and invited them to join in the festivities. The celebration continued with new energy and much laughter.

Suddenly a beat much stronger than that of Ermine's drum pulsed through the air. An enormous bird rose into the sky just as two youths emerged from the trees. Ermine recognized his brothers at once and ran to greet them. They had been released, just as the eagle-man and his mother had promised.

From then on, life was different. The people took the time to share and celebrate their blessings. They constructed new huts that stood side by side in a long row along the ocean's edge. Together they built a giant hall for feasts and festivals. Ermine decorated the building with intricate designs painted with brilliant colors. Soon the entire village was bright with painted carvings of fantastic animals and birds.

One day, Ermine walked out into the forest and followed the path leading to the mountains. As he had hoped, a giant eagle descended from the sky. Ermine and the eagle-man greeted each other warmly, then flew off together to the highest mountain peaks.

As they flew toward the eagles' home, the boy noticed another eagle spiraling downward. Within seconds, it joined them, gliding alongside. The bird's feathers shimmered in the sunlight, and her familiar eyes glowed with wisdom. With a flap of her newly powerful wings, the eagle-mother showed Ermine that she had received her gift. Through the warmth and energy created by the songs of his people, the ancient mother had become young again.